Digger and Skip!

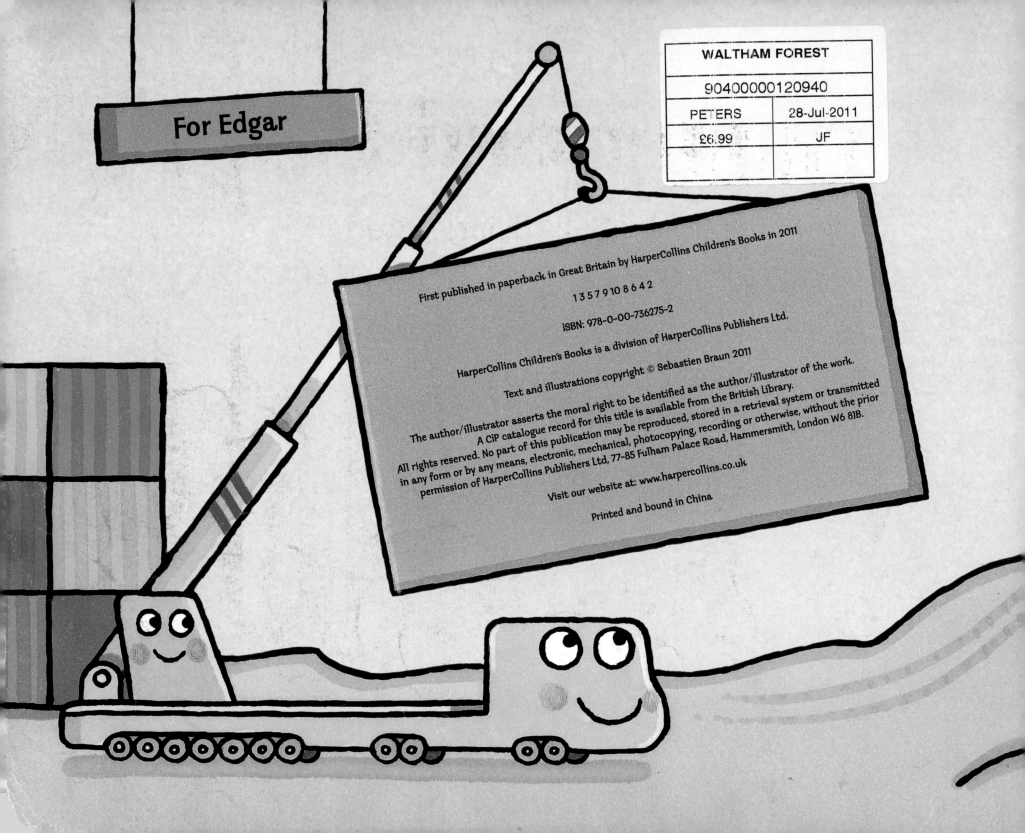

For Edgar

First published in paperback in Great Britain by HarperCollins Children's Books in 2011

1 3 5 7 9 10 8 6 4 2

iSBN: 978-0-00-736275-2

HarperCollins Children's Books is a division of HarperCollins Publishers Ltd.

Text and illustrations copyright © Sebastien Braun 2011

The author/illustrator asserts the moral right to be identified as the author/illustrator of the work.

A CiP catalogue record for this title is available from the British Library.

Visit our website at: www.harpercollins.co.uk

Printed and bound in China

Digger and Skip!

by Sebastien Braun

HarperCollins *Children's Books*

Dig!

Dig!

Dig!

This is Digger. Hello, Digger!
He is a very busy little digging machine.

Every day Digger tries his best to help out at the building site...

but things don't always
go quite to plan. "Uh-oh!"

One day Digger was tidying the building site
with his friend, Skip the dump truck.
"Just one more tiny rock left," said Skip.
"Easy," said Digger. "I'll get it!"

Just then, the other
machines gathered round.
"Leave the hard work to the experts now,
Digger," bossed Chuck the bulldozer.

"Let's take a break before we try again," said Chuck. "The building site's not safe if we leave the rock like this."

Skip looked at Digger...

"Why don't you
have another go?"
he whispered kindly.
"You're a digger. Digging's
what you do best!"

Dig!

And so, while
the others
rested, Digger
got to work.

He dug deeper...
and deeper...

Dig!

and deeper...

until, at last, the rock was free!
"You did it!"
cried Skip.

The other machines were amazed.
"Well done, Digger!" they cheered.

At last, they could finish
tidying the site... together.

Clank!

Clank!

Clank!

Heave!

Brrrm!

Brrrm!

It had been a long, hard day.
"What a team!"
said Skip.
"What fun!"
said Digger.

Tired but happy, Digger led his friends back home.

"Thank you for believing in me, Skip," said Digger,
as they settled down at the yard.

"Everyone in our team is special," said Skip,
"but we couldn't have done the job without you!"

Digger smiled sleepily...

"It's all in a day's work," he said.